"It's never happened to me before."

"I just froze," I admitted as we walked to the locker room.

"Well, welcome to the club," said Darlene.

"What club?" asked Becky. "The club of chickens?" She exploded into a laugh as if she had just said something hysterically funny. She started clucking like a chicken.

"Lay off, Becky," said Darlene. "You know you're not funny. And if anybody's not chicken, it's Jodi."

"Cluck, cluck," whispered Becky as she went into the shower.

Becky doesn't bother me. I just wish I knew why I was so scared of this one trick.

**Look for these and other books
in THE GYMNASTS series:**

THE GYMNASTS

#16 FEAR OF FALLING

Elizabeth Levy

AN
APPLE
PAPERBACK

SCHOLASTIC INC.
New York Toronto London Auckland Sydney

No part of this publication may be reproduced in whole or in part, or stored in a retrieval system, or transmitted in any form or by any means, electronic, mechanical, photocopying, recording, or otherwise, without written permission of the publisher. For information regarding permission, write to Scholastic Inc., 730 Broadway, New York, NY 10003.

ISBN 0-590-43834-4

Copyright © 1991 by Elizabeth Levy.
All rights reserved. Published by Scholastic Inc. APPLE PAPERBACKS is a registered trademark of Scholastic Inc. THE GYMNASTS is a trademark of Scholastic Inc.

12 11 10 9 8 7 6 5 4 3 2 1   1 2 3 4 5 6/9

Printed in the U.S.A.   28

First Scholastic printing, March 1991

*To Natan and Emma, and all
the twenty-first-century gymnasts.*

FEAR OF FALLING

Gymnast on Skateboard

If there is anything weirder than acquiring an instant family, I don't know what it is. I now have a little brother, Nick the Pest. I probably would never have even met him if our parents hadn't gotten married.

I was trying to teach Nick to jump the curb on the skateboard. I am a terrific skateboarder. I think it has to do with the fact that I've been doing gymnastics since I was a little kid and I have no fear. Some people are just born without fear. Nick, on the other hand, has a great imagination. He can imagine things to be afraid of that would never occur to me. He worries about tiny cracks in the sidewalk. He is absolutely positive that his wheels will catch in the cracks.

"Come on, Nick," I promised him. "I'll run alongside you to make sure that nothing happens. It'll be just like spotting you in the gym."

It was after supper, but it was still light out. I love evenings in late May and June when it seems to stay light forever. Mom and Barney were sitting under a shade tree in the front yard. We've moved out of our town house and into a big ranch house, just a couple of blocks from my teammate Darlene. It's only a one-story house, but it's got big front and back yards. Barney loves to garden, and the front yard is full of flowers.

I actually like the house, and I'm getting used to Mom being married. First of all, it's hard not to like Barney. He really is a nice man, and even I can see that Mom's happy.

Mom has blonde hair just like me, only she wears it short. The sun was shining on her hair, and it looked very pretty.

Mom's and Barney's heads were together, and they looked like they were having a serious discussion. Then Mom laughed. She's got a goofy laugh — almost a half-snort. It's kind of cute, and Barney makes her giggle and laugh more than anyone. Barney actually makes everybody laugh. He owns a chain of pet stores called Barking Barney's, and all his radio advertisements begin with a riddle. This week's riddle is, "What animals follow you wherever you go?" The answer is, "Your calves."

Barney is not athletic. He thinks that gardening is exercise. Mom never used to like to sit around. She's got more energy than even I do, and I have a *lot* of energy, but I've noticed lately that she loves to relax with Barney.

"Jodi," yelled Mom. "Shouldn't Nick have knee and elbow pads on?"

"Mom, we're not exactly breaking any speed records here or doing anything tricky," I said. "Poky Nick is only going about two miles an hour."

Nick sat down on his skateboard and put his chin in his hands.

"What's wrong?" I asked him.

"I don't like you calling me Poky Nick."

"You call me Jodi-podi all the time, and I don't complain."

"Yes, you do," said Nick.

"Get up," I said. "You gotta try it. Just bend your knees as you're about to go up the curb. It's a lot like punching off the springboard."

"I'm scared," Nick admitted. "I'm scared half the skateboard's going to go up the curb and the other half will stay down, and I'll fall."

I put my hands on my hips. I couldn't believe he was afraid of such a dinky trick. Nick's only eight years old and, honestly, sometimes I think he's scared of his own shadow.

"It's nothing to be afraid of," I told him. "Look!" I took the skateboard from him and rode it for a little momentum. Then I flipped the two front wheels in the air and jumped the curb.

"Nothing to it!"

"You say that about everything," whined Nick. I've got to confess that it felt great to be able to do things that Nick wouldn't dare. My older sister, Jennifer, is good at everything. She's in college now. She's in the Air Force Academy, and she wants to be an astronaut. She was a much better gymnast than I'll ever be. My dad lives back in St. Louis, and he runs a gymnastics center. I was always the worst athlete in our family until I acquired Nick.

Nick has gotten into gymnastics, but he works with our archrivals, the Atomic Amazons. It's okay. It's better than having him in *my* gym, the Evergreen Gymnastics Academy.

Nick got up and started scooting along the curb. I shouldn't have called it scooting — it was more like poking.

"Okay, *now*!" I shouted.

Nick chickened out. He looked back at me, a kind of pathetic look on his face.

"I don't see what you're scared of," I said. "It's just an itty-bitty curb. I'll show you again."

I picked up the skateboard and took it up the street a ways so I could get a good turn on it. I love the feeling when I'm going fast.

I saw a jogger coming around the corner, hugging the curb. She was really motoring, and I decided to wait until she passed so I wouldn't be in her way. Then I recognized her. It was Heidi Ferguson from our gym. She was wearing dark glasses and a baseball cap, and she was singing along at the top of her lungs to a song she was listening to on her earphones. Heidi is not at all the kind of gymnast who I'd imagine singing while she runs.

Usually Heidi is deadly serious about everything she does. She's an incredibly good gymnast. In fact, if she gets her act together, everybody is betting that she makes it to the Olympics.

"Heidi!" I shouted.

Heidi looked up. She pulled off her earphones and jogged in place in front of me.

"Hi, Jodi!" She grinned. She was glistening with sweat.

"Don't you get enough of a workout in the gym?" I asked her. Heidi spends about six hours a day in the gym. She doesn't go to school. She takes correspondence classes so that she can have time to train.

"Conditioning," said Heidi, hardly even panting. "What are you doing on *that*?"

She looked at my skateboard as if it were pond scum on wheels.

"I'm about to show my little brother how to make this thing fly," I said.

"You? On a skateboard?" asked Heidi. "I don't believe it."

"Oh, yeah?" I said. "Watch this!"

I took off down the hill, dipping, trying to look like a surfer catching a wave. I was showing off, and when I hit the curb, I flipped the skateboard too high. The wheels spun out from under me, but I fell so that I landed on my side. One thing about gymnastics — it sure teaches you how to fall.

Heidi, Nick, Mom, and Barney ran up to me. "Are you okay?" Nick asked. He looked at my elbow. "Oh, yuck!" he said.

My elbow was scraped and bleeding. "It's not so bad."

"That's why you'd *never* catch me on one of those," said Heidi. "And I think *you're* foolish to get on one."

"What do you mean?" I asked. "You fall off the beam and the high bar. I just fell a couple of inches."

"But that's gymastics," said Heidi. "I would never risk hurting myself doing something so silly as skateboarding."

"Heidi's right," said Mom. "When I was competing, I wasn't allowed to ski or roller-skate."

"Well, I'm not some coddled egg," I said. I picked up my skateboard.

"I've got to keep on running," said Heidi. "I don't want to cool down. You sure you're okay, Jodi?"

"Yeah," I said, rubbing my elbow. It did sting.

"See you in the gym," said Heidi.

"I think she's so cool," said Nick. "I can't believe she works out in your gym."

"Neither can anybody else," I muttered. Mom and Barney had gone back to sitting on the lounge chairs. They were whispering something to each other. Then Mom waved.

"Jodi, Nick, come over here. There's something that Barney and I want to talk to you about."

My friend Lauren Baca says it's a proven fact that "there's something I want to talk to you about" are the most frightening words in the English language.

"Uh-oh," I said to Nick. "What did you do now?"

"I didn't do a thing," protested Nick.

"Well, I sure hope it's not something I did," I said.

2

Cats Have It Easy

"You're what?" I exclaimed. Nick stared at Mom's belly as if he expected an alien little brother or sister to come out of it at any moment.

"Aren't you guys too old for this?" Nick whispered. I could have hugged him. That's exactly what I was thinking, but I was afraid to say it out loud.

"I'm not too old," said Mom. "I've got to admit that I didn't expect this. We didn't plan to have a baby, but Barney and I have talked and talked about it, and we're both excited. We waited to tell you, because I know you've had so much to adjust to. But we can't wait any longer. I'm beginning to show."

I looked at Mom. She didn't even look pregnant. "You're not about to have the baby right away," I said.

Mom laughed. "No, not for many months yet."

"Mom, it's ridiculous," I said. "I mean, you've got one kid at the Air Force Academy. . . . How's it going to look if you go to Jennifer's graduation next year with a tiny baby?"

"Who cares how it looks," said Mom, "as long as we love each other?"

I rolled my eyes. Ever since she's gotten married, Mom has had a disturbing tendency to sound like a goopy country-and-western song.

"I know this is a shock for you kids," said Barney. "It took me a while to get used to the idea, but I think it will be fun. Think of the things you two will be able to teach the baby."

"I can't even teach Nick how to skateboard," I said. "How do you expect me to teach a baby anything?"

Mom reached over and pushed my hair away from my forehead. "Jodi, you'll have so much to teach him or her."

"Speaking of him or her, do you know what it is? Do I have to get ready for *another* boy?" I asked.

"It'd better be a boy," said Nick. "I need a little male support around here."

Barney laughed. "We decided we didn't want to know," he said.

"What do you mean, 'didn't want to know'?" I asked.

"Well, the doctors know. Because your mom's past thirty-five, they do tests to make sure everything is all right. They actually take pictures of the baby."

"Oh, gross," said Nick.

"It was kind of neat," said Barney.

"And you mean they could actually see already whether it was a boy or a girl?" I asked.

"No, that was another test," said Mom. "But the doctor *does* know what sex the baby is. Barney and I asked her not to tell us."

"Some doctor knows whether I'm going to have a brother or sister, and I don't?" yelled Nick. "That's not fair."

I couldn't agree more, but I kept my mouth shut. It was great having Nick say all the things that I couldn't or wouldn't say. I get to be the voice of reason, which, believe me, is a new experience for me.

"Nick, it'll be so much more fun if it's a surprise," Mom said.

"This is enough of a surprise," I muttered.

Mom frowned. She reached out for my hand. "I don't blame you for being shocked. It's a surprise for all of us. But I know you, and you're going to be a great older sister."

"Yeah, she's got me to practice on," said Nick.

"I've never had a younger anything."

"Have you told Patrick yet?" I asked Mom. Patrick is my coach at the gym, and he's Mom's boss.

"No, I wanted you to be the first to know after Barney," said Mom. "I'll tell Patrick on Monday. I'd like to keep working at the gym, but I won't be able to do any heavy lifting. Maybe I'll be able to help Patrick with the clerical work."

"Clerical work. You're a coach, not a clerk."

"I know, Jodi. But at my age, it's not as simple as when I had you. I have to be careful."

I couldn't imagine Mom being careful. She was the one who would always dare to try anything.

Sar-Cat, my cat, was stalking something across the lawn. Cats have it easy. They just live by instinct. They aren't born into complicated families. If Sar-Cat had any stepbrothers or -sisters, he didn't know about them. I would have liked it that way.

3

I Love the Pit

"A baby will be so cute," said Ti An Truong, one of the youngest members of my team. She's nine. "I'll bet Barney gets it a new puppy as soon as it's born."

"Great, then I'll have to help take care of a new puppy and a new baby at the same time. That's all I'll need."

On Monday afternoon, I had told my teammates first thing, while we were changing into our leotards in the locker room. My team is called the Pinecones, because we're from the Evergreen Gymnastics Academy. Patrick gave us the name a long time ago. Sometimes I wish we had a zippier name like the Amazons or the Supertwisters, but I've never wished for a better team. We may not collect many trophies, but we're best friends.

I know enough not to keep anything that is bothering me from my teammates. I had tried that once, and it had been a disaster.

"I think it's wonderful that your mom's having a baby," said Darlene. Darlene Broderick would say that. Darlene is probably the nicest kid on our team. She's the oldest, and she's not wishy-washy nice; she's genuinely nice. Her dad is "Big Beef" Broderick, a football player for the Denver Broncos.

"Darlene, you've already got two younger sisters — you know what to do with them," I said.

"Isn't your mom awfully old to be having a baby?" asked Heidi. "I mean, your sister will be graduating from the Air Force Academy soon."

"It's a proven fact that women can have babies well into their forties," said Lauren. "Jodi's mom is — "

"Forty-one," I said. "She's forty-one."

"Well, I think it's neat," said Darlene. "Don't worry, Jodi. When the time comes I'll teach you all about changing diapers."

"Oh, great," I said. "That sounds like so much fun."

"Admit it," said Darlene. "You're a little excited about it. Babies are terrific."

"I'm not excited. I'm still in shock," I said. "Having Nick the Pest has been strange enough."

"Yeah, but this baby will know you from the minute it's born. It's different," said Darlene.

"I certainly hope so," I said.

We went out into the gym. The best thing about Heidi Ferguson working out in our gym was that we had recently gotten a foam pit. I love working out over the foam pit. It's a big pit filled with squares of foam. The foam pit makes me feel like I can do anything without hurting myself. I can do tricks into the foam pit that I'd be crazy to even try on the regular beam or bars.

It's a blast to work on, especially if you're like me and actually *like* falling. There're kids like Ti An who are timid, and for them the pit is terrific because it gives them confidence. I like the pit because it's fun.

We finished our warm-ups. Patrick told us we were going to work on our beam dismounts.

"Over the foam pit?" I asked.

Patrick nodded. "I knew that would make you happy. We're going to learn the roundoff to a back-somersault dismount."

14

Darlene whistled and shook her hand up and down. "Pretty impressive."

"I think you girls are ready for it," said Patrick.

Darlene scrunched up her eyes as if she couldn't believe she'd be ready for such a complicated move. The truth was that all of us had been improving the last few months. Lauren was sure it was Heidi's influence, and I think she's right. It's hard to be around somebody who works as hard as Heidi and not notch up a little in your own work.

"Okay," said Patrick. "Jodi, you go first."

"Can I do it on the beam in the pit?" I asked Patrick.

Patrick nodded. "In the beginning, but remember, eventually you've got to do it on the regular beam."

" 'The purpose of the pit is just for learning,' " Darlene and I repeated in unison. " 'It's not an amusement park.' "

Patrick laughed. "Do I really say that all the time?" he asked.

All the Pinecones nodded. I think Patrick loved having the pit as much as we did.

Patrick diagrammed the move for us. A round-off is just a cartwheel with a turn in it so you end up facing the way you started. It's a real beginner's move, *except* when you've got to land on four inches of beam. Then it's not so easy.

I climbed onto the beam over the pit and got my balance. I jumped into the roundoff. When I was upside down, I couldn't see how far I was from the end of the beam. The next thing I knew I was falling sideways. I should have just jumped into the pit — that's what it was there for — but instead I tried to regain my balance. I came crashing down, scraping the beam with the small of my back.

"Ouch!" I yelled as I slipped into the pit. My eyes were stinging with tears. I had hit my coccyx, the hard bone at the end of the spinal column.

Patrick dropped his clipboard and held his hand out over the pit to help me up.

"Are you okay?" he asked.

I nodded yes, but I was lying. My back really hurt. I was going to be black and blue.

"Do you want to know what you did wrong?" Heidi asked.

"That's my least favorite question in the world!" I snapped.

Patrick put a hand on Heidi's shoulder. "It's okay, Heidi. Let's give Jodi a chance to catch her breath. Do you want to put an ice pack on your back?" he asked me.

I shook my head. "No, I'm fine," I said. "I just slipped."

"Are you sure you're okay?" Patrick asked again.

I nodded. Patrick smiled at me. He knows I'm tough. "Go stand back in line," he said. "You can try it again."

I went to stand behind Lauren who was last in line. "That hurt just to watch," she said.

"It hurt me more," I admitted. I rubbed my coccyx. It was good and sore.

I watched as Darlene and then Ti An, Ashley, and Cindi tried the roundoff on the beam that was going to lead to doing a back somersault off the beam. Each of them fell, too, but when they fell they landed in the soft foam. Nobody else hit the beam.

Lauren went next, and she never made it to the somersault. She slipped doing the roundoff just like me, but she fell over laughing into the foam pit.

I was supposed to go next. Darlene nudged me.

"You go," I said. "I've got to go to the bathroom."

Darlene nodded. I told Patrick why I was leaving the room. I ran into the locker room. I splashed cold water on my face. I took off my leotard and twisted around to see my back. It was already red.

I took an extra long time in the bathroom. When I came back out, Patrick had moved us over to the mats to practice our floor exercises. I was relieved we weren't doing the beam anymore. I'd had more than enough for one day. In fact, I'd had more than enough for quite a while.

I Hate This Move

Sometimes it takes us months to learn a new trick. This was certainly true of the roundoff somersault beam dismount. It gets boring, especially if you aren't getting it, like me. The move just continued to give me trouble.

Meanwhile Mom was definitely getting a big belly. She still came to the gym, but she wasn't coaching much. She spent a lot of time putting our schedule on the new computer that Patrick had bought. He had also hired a new assistant coach for the boys' team. He was a friend of Patrick's from college, Gerald Jackson, who was the weirdest gymnastics coach I had ever seen. He was *tall*. Most gymnasts, even the guys, are small, but Gerald apparently was a great high school gymnast, and then he had a growth spurt in college.

Cindi's brother Jared told us that the guys really liked him, and Mom seemed to like him, too.

Mom came over to Patrick with a computer printout. She smiled at me. I still couldn't get used to how strange she looked pregnant. When she sat down, she had no lap left.

Patrick took the printout from Mom. "We're going to practice our beam dismounts today," he said. "We're almost ready to do the roundoff somersault without the pit."

I groaned.

"Jodi, was that groan from you?" asked Patrick.

"I hate this trick," I said. "I'm never going to get it." I regretted the words as soon as they were out of my mouth. Patrick doesn't like us to say "never."

"Never?" repeated Patrick. "Come on, Jodi. You can do a roundoff on the beam. You can do a somersault dismount. It's just a question of putting the pieces together."

"Oh, right," I said sarcastically. "Putting the pieces together on four inches of beam isn't so easy."

"I know," said Patrick. "However, the trick is to try for a smooth transition between the two moves. It looks a lot harder than it is."

"Easy for you to say," I muttered. "You don't have to do it."

"I'll let someone else show you," said Patrick. "Heidi, would you mind demonstrating a round-off back-somersault dismount for us?"

"No problem," said Heidi. She put her hands on the beam, swung her legs into a sitting position, and then stood up. It always surprises me how Heidi rarely shows off. You'd think with all of us watching her, she'd do a complicated mount up onto the beam, even though Patrick hadn't asked her to. I've seen some of the mounts to the beam that Heidi could do in competition, and awesome isn't the word for them. Yet in practice, she just puts her hands on the beam and pushes up.

Heidi stood up on the beam and twisted her neck a little bit to release the tension. She shook her hands. You could see her eyes focusing on the end of the beam.

She walked to the end and measured off the distance she would need to do the trick. Then she took a deep breath and let the air out. She threw her arms into the air. Her arms were like steel rods as she jumped into the roundoff, pushing off upside down from the beam.

She snapped her legs in the air. I could hear the thunk as she landed with both feet solidly

21

on the beam. She immediately lifted her arms again and tucked off the end of the beam. It had seemed like she hadn't even looked to make sure she was on the end. She did a double back somersault into the pit. She landed with such power that the chunks of foam flew into the air around her.

Patrick was laughing. "I only asked for a single back," he said.

Heidi grinned. "I couldn't resist," she said. "That's the dismount I'm going to do at the world championships."

"Oh, great," said Ti An. "And you expect us to do that?"

"Not exactly the double back," said Patrick. "But you all saw how quickly Heidi got her hands up in the air after she landed the roundoff. That's the trick to it.

"Okay, Jodi. You try it. But just a single somersault after the roundoff, please."

"No problem," I joked.

Heidi climbed out of the pit and stood at the side watching me.

I pushed up onto the beam, exactly the way Heidi did. I figured if it was good enough for her, it was good enough for me.

I put my hands over my head. I kicked upside down into the roundoff, but when I was upside down, I suddenly got scared to land on my feet.

I pictured myself landing on my head. I panicked and fell, forgetting to protect myself, and I hit my tailbone on the beam again!

It hurt like the dickens. Patrick gave me a concerned look. "You okay?" he asked.

"I hate this move!" I said.

"Me, too," said Lauren.

I pulled myself out of the pit and rubbed my back.

"You'll get it," said Patrick.

I watched Lauren try for it. She wobbled landing on her roundoff, but she punched up into the back somersault. I could tell that she'd be ready to do it without the pit any day now. I didn't even want to think about doing that move without the safety of the pit. In fact, I'd be happy never to think about that move again. Unfortunately, I knew Patrick would never rest easy until I learned it.

5

I Wish It Were
a Scary Movie

I didn't turn just black and blue from my latest fall off the beam. I turned purple and green. For a while my back looked like an underripe eggplant. Now that the bruise was finally fading it had turned yellowish. I was at home on a Saturday morning, looking at the remains of the bruise in the mirror, when I heard Mom yell for me.

It wasn't her normal yell. She didn't sound panicked, but she didn't sound right. I know all the ways Mom yells my name. There's the "*Jodi!*" when I've done something wrong, and "*Jo — di*" when she's cheering me on. But this sounded different.

I ran into her bedroom. Mom was lying in bed. She looked big under the sheet. She also looked worried.

"Mom?" I asked. "Is something wrong?"

Mom licked her lips. It was a silly question. I knew something was wrong by the expression on her face.

"Honey, can you bring the phone over here?" she asked.

I stared at her. The phone was only on the other side of the bed. Barney had left for work early. He often gets to the pet stores way before they open. He likes to supervise the feeding of his pets. Barney feels responsible for every animal under his care.

Mom grimaced. I grabbed the phone. "Mom! What's wrong? Should I call 911?"

"No, no, it's not an emergency. It's just that I've been having cramps all night, and I need to call the doctor."

Mom is almost never sick.

"I didn't want to move around any more than is necessary," she said. "It hurts when I move. Jodi, don't look so worried."

I thought that was the silliest thing Mom had ever told me. I couldn't help but look worried.

Mom punched in her doctor's number. I held her hand. Mom smiled at me. She really didn't look very sick. She hung up the phone.

"The doctor's coming right over," she said. "She said I did the right thing to stay in bed. It's nothing to panic about, Jodi. It's just that Doctor Potler told me that because of my age, I should let her know immediately if I had any labor pains."

"You mean you could have the baby right now?" I said, my voice rising.

"Jodi . . . no . . . we're not going to do the scene from *Gone With the Wind*, I promise." *Gone With the Wind* is Mom's favorite movie. She makes me watch it every time it's on TV, and my least favorite scene is the one where Miss Melanie is having a baby. I knew *nothing* about birthing babies, but I did know I wanted Mom to have this baby in a hospital with a zillion doctors and nurses around.

"Do you want me to call Barney?" I asked Mom.

"I'll call his office," said Mom. "They'll know where he is." Mom got a hold of Barney. She whispered into the phone. She didn't exactly sound as if she were telling Barney that it was nothing. Mom hung up and saw me staring at her.

"Jodi, there's no reason to panic. Doctor Potler said she'd be here in just a few minutes."

"That's the second time you've told me not to panic," I said. "It must mean it's serious."

When the doorbell rang, I opened the door for Doctor Potler.

I took her to Mom's bedroom. Mom looked a little better. "Jodi, I'll examine your mother," said Doctor Potler. "Why don't you wait in your room? There's no need to panic."

Every time someone said that to me, I panicked a little bit more.

I heard a car speed into the driveway. Barney came rushing through the door. "How is she?" he asked.

"Doctor Potler's with Mom," I said. "Everybody says not to panic."

Barney patted me on the shoulder. "Good," he said. I didn't know what was good about it. Barney went to their room.

I paced around the living room. Sar-Cat seemed to sense that I was upset. He stared at me from a chair across the room.

The phone rang. I rushed to pick it up. I thought maybe Doctor Potler had called for an ambulance.

"Yo, Jodi," said Darlene, sounding incredibly cheerful. It was strange to hear somebody's voice who genuinely didn't sound worried.

"Hi," I said.

"Are you okay?" Darlene asked, sensing immediately that something *was* wrong. That's one of the things I love most about Darlene.

"It's Mom," I said.

"The baby?" Darlene asked.

"I don't know," I admitted. "The doctor's upstairs with her."

"You aren't alone, are you?" Darlene asked. "Do you want me to come over?"

"No, Barney's here," I said. "Everybody's telling me not to panic."

"That must make you feel great," said Darlene sarcastically.

I laughed. It was great to be talking to Darlene.

"Yeah," I muttered.

"Well, I'm here if you need me," said Darlene. "I was just calling to ask if you wanted a ride to the gym. We're supposed to have practice at eleven this morning."

"I don't know," I said. "I think I'd better stick around here."

"Well, you can call if you need me," said Darlene.

I wished I knew what was happening. I wished it *were* a movie. I *like* scary movies. I like them just because I know it's all pretend. I know that at the end of two hours I'll know exactly how it's going to come out. But this wasn't a movie. Nobody knew how it was going to come out.

Barney came out into the living room.

"Is Mom all right?" I asked him. Barney tried to smile at me, but it wasn't a very relaxed smile.

"She's fine," he said. "The doctor's just being cautious. We're going to the hospital for some tests."

"What kind of tests?" I asked.

"We just have to be sure that the baby's all right. But it's nothing to worry about." Barney sounded worried. "Your mom said you were terrific," he said.

"All I did was get the telephone for her," I insisted.

"Yes, but you did that very well," said Barney. He grinned. I could tell that he was teasing, and it made me feel a little better that Barney could still make a joke.

"I'm sure the judges would have given me a 9.6 for picking up the telephone," I said sarcastically.

Just then, Mom and the doctor came out of the bedroom. Mom was dressed in a red warm-up suit, and seeing her standing up and dressed made me feel a lot better. Just the fact that she had taken the time to pick out her favorite color made me think that things couldn't be serious.

"Okay," said the doctor. "Why don't I follow you to the hospital in my car? You can go straight to the third floor. You don't have to go to the emergency room or anything."

I went into my closet and got my jacket.

"Jodi," said Mom, "you don't have to come to the hospital. You have practice later this morning."

"Yeah, Mom . . . but," I stammered.

"We're just taking your mom in for some tests for the baby," said Doctor Potler. "Sometimes women who are older have premature labor and need to be extra careful to hold on to the baby. This is for routine monitoring."

"Mom, do you feel better?" I asked.

"Much," said Mom. "And I want to thank you. You did just great."

It was still making me a little bit nervous the way that everyone was telling me how great I was.

"Do you have a way of getting to the gym?" Barney asked me.

"Darlene will pick me up," I said, but I was still worried.

Mom could read my mind. "Jodi, there's nothing to worry about. I've got Barney and Doctor Potler. I'll be home when you get back from the gym, and everything will be fine."

I looked from Mom to the doctor.

"Your mother's telling you the truth," said Doctor Potler.

Barney put his arm around Mom. "Jodi, remember, don't worry. We'll let you know if anything's wrong."

"Yeah, right," I said. I worried right until the moment that Darlene came to pick me up. The more people told me not to worry, the scarier it got.

Freeze

"Is your mom doing okay?" Darlene's mom asked me. Mrs. Broderick is a beautiful woman who still models occasionally. It's hard to believe she's the mother of three kids.

"I think so," I said. "They went to the hospital for some tests. Everybody tells me not to worry."

"I hate that," said Darlene.

I poked her in the arm. "Me, too," I said.

"Well, I remember my last pregnancy," said Mrs. Broderick. "I had to have a zillion checkups, but everything went fine."

"Don't worry," said Darlene and I in unison.

Mrs. Broderick laughed. "I guess you kids get tired of hearing us say that all the time. But honestly, Jodi, I'm sure everything will be just fine."

"Right," I said.

Mrs. Broderick let us off in front of the gym. Becky Dyson was being let off at the same time. Becky Dyson is snotty, egotistical, and nasty, and that's just for starters. She was also the best gymnast in our gym until Heidi started working out with us.

"Hi, Darlene. Hi, Jodi," said Becky in her peculiar drawl. I think she's trying to sound like she's upper-class. Instead she just sounds like she didn't quite finish swallowing her breakfast. "What's new?"

I didn't feel like telling Becky my problems. "Nothing," I said quickly.

"What's wrong with her?" Becky asked Darlene. "All I did was say hello."

Becky did have a point. "Sorry I snapped at you," I said to her.

"Well, it's no skin off my nose," said Becky. Darlene and I looked at each other. Even when I tried to be nice to Becky, it backfired.

We went into the gym, and I was in a better mood. Having things be normally nasty with Becky helped me forget being worried about my mom.

I changed into my leotard. I loosened up during

my warm-ups. First we worked on our tumbling passes on the floor. I was glad to be moving. The best thing about gymnastics is that it's hard to be worried and do a double flip.

Patrick patted me on the back after my last tumbling pass. "Jodi, you're really flying."

I was breathing too hard to say thank you, but I grinned at him.

"Okay, girls, let's work on the beam," said Patrick. He blew his whistle.

I headed for the pits. Patrick stopped me. "It's time to try it on the regulation beam," he said. "You've had enough practice in the pits."

I knew it had to happen sometime.

Becky was working on the beam with Heidi watching her. She looked annoyed when we came over. "I'm not through," Becky complained.

"We have to give the Pinecones a chance," said Patrick. "It's your turn to work on your tumbling pass on the floor."

"I'll stay and watch the Pinecones," said Heidi.

Becky put her hands on her hips. "I *need* you to watch me," she said.

Heidi shook her head. "After I watch the Pinecones," she said. "I want to see how they do on their new dismount now that they're trying it for real. They're doing the roundoff somie dismount."

Becky shifted her weight impatiently from one

foot to the other. "That's what I was working on," she said. "The Pinecones aren't good enough to do that!"

"Yes, they are," said Patrick.

I yawned.

"Jodi," asked Patrick, "am I boring you?"

"Sorry," I said quickly. "I don't know why I did that." I yawned again. I couldn't help myself.

"Remember, we're going to be . . ." Patrick paused. I had yawned again.

"Jodi, did you get enough sleep?" he asked me.

I felt myself blush. "Sure," I said. My hands were sweating.

"Is anything wrong?" Darlene asked me.

I twisted my neck around. The muscles around my shoulders felt stiff. I could hear a crackle as I cocked my head to one side.

I yawned again. Then I raised my hand. "Patrick, I have to go to the bathroom," I said.

Patrick glanced up at me. "Sure, Jodi. Come right back."

I ran as fast as I could into the locker room. I peed and then splashed cold water on my face. My lips looked pale. And my heart was beating faster than normal. I licked my lips and went back out into the gym.

I was very glad to be at the end of the line. I yawned another time. Ti An was in front of me, and she looked as nervous as I was. "I just know

I'm going to fall," she said to me in a worried voice.

"Ti An, you can't think like that," I said. "You gotta just go for it. You're really good."

"No, I'm not," said Ti An. "I'm not like you."

"What do you mean?" I asked. "I'm the one who's sweating like a pig."

"Pigs don't sweat," said Ti An. "Remember, Lauren taught us that."

"Yeah, right," I said, rubbing my hands on my legs.

"Okay, Ti An," said Patrick. "It's your turn."

"I'm scared," said Ti An.

"Ti An, what are you scared about?" Patrick asked.

"Landing on the roundoff," said Ti An. "I'm not scared of doing the back-somersault dismount. It's just that I'm scared I'll miss the beam on the roundoff."

Ti An was a little kid, but she was honest and smart. I don't think I would have ever been able to just tell Patrick that I was afraid — much less to tell him exactly what I feared.

"That's okay, Ti An," said Patrick. "Doing a roundoff on the beam *is* scary. But you've done it lots of times before into the pit. I'll be here to spot you. Don't slow it down just because you're worried about the landing."

Ti An bit her lip. She nodded. She mounted

the beam and raised her hands over her head to begin the roundoff. Then she lit into the move, snapping her legs together at the top of the cartwheel and coming down solidly. She punched up and threw herself backward into the somersault. Patrick just had to touch her back to help her around, and she landed on the mats.

"That's it, Ti An!" said Patrick.

Ti An grinned at him. Ti An was like that. She looked timid and afraid. Yet when the screws were down she could be an absolute tiger in learning a new trick. Then she'd lose it again all over in competition. But she was getting better and better. She used to be anxious all the time, and she couldn't plug it in when it counted. Now, Ti An still *said* she was anxious, but she could do it.

"Jodi, my girl, it's your turn," said Patrick. "Remember what I said to Ti An — you can't slow down the roundoff. You've got to really punch it out."

I climbed onto the beam. I had known all along that the foam pit was just for practice. Usually I like to go cold turkey on a trick. I don't like it when Patrick tries to dissect a move for me. There's such a thing as thinking too much. I couldn't worry just about slowing down the roundoff. I had the somersault to do, too. I just wanted to do it.

I got up on the beam. Heidi stood to the side, watching me. Becky was just a step behind her, watching, too. I knew Becky was hoping I'd fall again. She wasn't happy with the way the Pinecones were improving.

Heidi was smiling at me. I knew that she was hoping I'd hit the beam squarely. Heidi's not like Becky. She doesn't like to see me fail.

I raised my arms to start my roundoff. My neck felt so tight. It felt as if it were screwed onto my head wrong. I twisted it around to loosen it.

"Come on, Jodi," urged Patrick. "Just remember to snap your legs together at the top. Keep your head down as you're doing the roundoff."

I took a deep breath and jumped into my cartwheel. I couldn't see where the end of the beam was. I was sure that I was going to miss it. I lifted my head and immediately fell sideways off the beam onto the mat. I didn't hurt myself.

I giggled. Then I started laughing so hard that I hiccupped.

"What's so funny?" Patrick asked me.

I could feel myself turn red. "Sorry," I said, but I couldn't stop giggling.

Patrick was looking at me strangely. It really wasn't funny.

"Jodi, try it again," he said softly.

I nodded.

I walked around to the side of the beam and

mounted it. I kept my eye on the end of the beam as I started to kick into my cartwheel. Then I froze. My mind told my body to keep moving. My body screamed "No!"

Patrick came to the side of the beam. "What's wrong?" he asked.

I knew I was beet-red. "I don't think I can do it," I said. "I'm sure I'm going to fall on my head."

"Okay," said Patrick softly. "Come on down. You'll do it tomorrow."

"Right," I said.

Patrick patted me on the back. "Jodi, don't worry about it," he said. "You had a great day, up till now. You'll get this trick."

I sighed. I wasn't worried until the moment that Patrick told me not to worry. I had had enough of adults telling me not to worry.

7

Something Weird Going On

"That's never happened to me. I just froze," I admitted as we walked to the locker room.

"Don't worry about it," said Cindi.

"That's what Patrick said, but — "

"Hey," said Cindi, poking me in the arm, "we've all had those moments."

"Not me," I said.

"Well, welcome to the club," said Darlene.

"What club?" asked Becky. "The club of chickens?" She exploded into a laugh as if she had just said something hysterically funny. She started clucking like a chicken.

"Go lay an egg," I said.

"You're the chicken who should know how to do that!" said Becky.

"Lay off, Becky," said Darlene. "You know you're not funny. And if anybody's not chicken, it's Jodi."

"Cluck, cluck," whispered Becky as she went into the shower.

"Don't let her bother you," said Lauren.

"I won't," I said. "She doesn't bother me. I just wish I knew why I'm so scared of this one trick."

"Maybe you're worried about your mom," suggested Darlene.

"Oh, please, Darlene," I begged. Darlene was always looking for the deeper meaning in things. I know she means well, but sometimes it gets to be a little too much. "This is gymnastics, not a soap opera," I reminded her.

"What's wrong with Jodi's mom?" Ti An asked.

"Nothing," I said. "She just had to see the doctor this morning and then go to the hospital for some tests."

"That's scary," said Ti An. It would help sometimes if Ti An weren't quite so honest about what she is feeling.

"Jodi, do you want us to come home with you?" Darlene asked. "I could wait with you if your mom isn't back yet."

"I'm not doing anything this afternoon, either," said Cindi.

"Me neither," said Lauren.

"I've got piano lessons," said Ti An.

"I've got to go to my grandma's," said Ashley.

"Hey, this isn't a crisis. My mom's not sick; she's just pregnant."

"Dad's picking us up," said Darlene. "He'll drive you home." Big Beef was waiting when we got out of the gym. We piled into the Brodericks' Bronco with Big Beef driving. Big Beef always cheers me up. He weighs about two hundred and sixty pounds. He's six foot three, and he's all muscle. You'd think he'd be scary, but he's got a big grin, and he loves the Pinecones. He thinks we've been terrific for Darlene. Before she met us, Darlene didn't trust many people. She thought everyone wanted to get to know her because of her dad.

"Hi, Jodi," he said to me. "I understand that you're about to get a baby brother or sister. Which is it?"

"Nobody knows but the doctor," I said. "And she's not telling."

"Which do you want it to be?" Big Beef asked me.

I realized I didn't care as much as I thought. Before I was sure that I wanted it to be a girl. Now I just wanted it to be all right. "Whatever," I said.

"I think you're taking it very well," said Big Beef. "You've had a lot of changes all at once. I wouldn't have liked it when I was your age."

"Dad," said Darlene. "Jodi's really excited about the baby."

Big Beef winked at me. I really like Big Beef. He made me feel better.

We pulled up in front of our new house. Both Barney's and Mom's cars were in the garage. I was relieved that they were back.

"They're home," I said to everybody. "You don't have to come in."

"Do you want us to?" asked Darlene.

I shook my head. "Naw," I said. "It's not a big deal."

"Well, call us if you need us," said Big Beef.

"Right . . ." I said. I walked up the front steps. Nick was sitting in the living room. Usually he's got a million things that he's just *got* to do. Now, he was just sitting in the living room, as if he didn't know what to do with himself.

"How's Mom?" I asked him.

"Weird," he said.

"Weird?" I asked. "She's okay, isn't she?"

Nick shrugged. He looked a little weird himself. "Nick, tell me what's wrong."

"Nothing's wrong," he said. "That's what Dad says."

"Then why did you say 'weird'?" I wanted to strangle him.

Just then Barney came out of the bedroom. "Oh, Jodi," he said, as if he were surprised to see me. "You're home."

"What's wrong with Mom?" I said.

"Nothing," said Barney. "She's in bed."

"She's going to stay there," said Nick. He gave a nervous giggle.

"What does that mean?" I asked.

"Uh . . ." Barney stammered. It wasn't like him at all. "Come on, Jodi," he said. "Let's go see your mom."

There was definitely something weird going on.

8

Born Spoiled

Mom was sitting up in bed. She had the telephone by her side, and the entire bed was covered with books and magazines. She grinned at me when she saw me at the door. She looked a lot better than she had that morning.

"Hi, Mom," I said. "What's up?"

Mom patted the bed beside her. "Come sit down. I'll tell you what's going on. But the important thing for you to keep in mind is that I'm not sick, and I'm not in any danger."

"How long do you have to stay in bed?" I asked.

"That's what's going on. I'm going to be here for a long time. I can't get out of bed for a couple of months!"

My mouth dropped open. "A couple of

months!" I exclaimed. I turned around and stared at Barney. He got a foolish expression on his face. "Doctor's orders," he said.

"Barney," said Mom, "let me talk to Jodi alone."

Barney left the room. I was scared. If Mom had to stay in bed for a couple of months, she must really be in trouble. Maybe she *was* way too old to be having a baby.

I looked over at Mom's dresser. She kept a collage of pictures of Jennifer and me from the time we were little. I glanced into the half-opened door of Mom's closet. I wanted to look anywhere except at Mom's stomach.

"Jodi," said Mom, "I'm going to be fine. I'm not sick."

"Then why do you have to stay in bed?" I asked.

"I went into a form of early labor this morning," she said.

"What does 'early labor' mean?"

"It means that I was starting to push the baby out before its time to be born," Mom explained. "I could lose the baby. Doctor Potler wants me to be extra careful not to jostle the baby too much. This isn't that unusual. I've had this happen to friends of mine before. If I'm careful, everything should be fine."

"But . . . who's going to cook our meals and what about your work and . . . ?"

"Barney's a better cook than I am," Mom said.

She was right on that count. "And Barney's going to get me a laptop computer. I'll be able to put all of Patrick's records for the teams on the computer. I can work out diagrams for all the new USGF routines. It's amazing what you can do these days. In fact, I'm already hooked up to a computer. Doctor Potler is using real space-age technology to help me. I'll show you."

Mom was sounding as if it were all some kind of adventure. She pulled down the covers. She had a strap across her belly with a kind of square block buckling it together. The buckle had two indented circles right at the top above her belly button. It looked like a control panel from an airplane had landed on Mom's belly.

"What's that?" I asked.

"It's a monitor for the baby's heartbeat," said Mom. "I have to wear it for an hour at a time, and it keeps track of every heartbeat with a tiny computer chip . . . and then . . . hand me the phone."

"The baby needs to make a phone call?" I joked.

"Exactly," said Mom. She took the phone receiver and laid it on the square.

"It's a modem," said Mom. She punched out some numbers on the phone. "It's connected to the hospital's computer so that Doctor Potler can read the results."

"Great," I muttered. "The kid isn't even born yet, and already she's hogging the phone."

"Or he," said Mom. "Isn't modern technology amazing?"

"Yes," I said. "The baby's going to be a space cadet."

"I think the science of it is fascinating," said Mom.

"If it's so high-tech, you'd think they'd figure out a more efficient way of having babies," I said.

Mom laughed. "Jodi, the point is that I'm going to be fine. The baby's going to be fine. I just have to be very careful not to move around too much. I don't want to go into labor before the baby's ready."

"You really have to stay in bed the whole time?" I asked.

"Pretty much," said Mom. "I can take a quick shower, but I have to dry off in bed. I have to try to keep the baby as stable as possible. In the end it'll be worth it. You were worth it."

"I didn't make you stay in bed for two months," I said. "You always told us how when you were pregnant with me and Jennifer you were still up on the beam."

"Well, this baby is going to be different," said Mom.

"Yeah, she'll probably expect breakfast in bed

her whole life," I said. "And she'll probably want me to bring it to her."

"Or him," Mom said automatically. The contraption around her belly began to beep.

"See," I said. "That's him now, calling for room service."

Mom cracked up. "Jodi, with a sister like you, I'm sure this baby's going to be okay. The beep just means that the monitor went through to the hospital's computer and everything's fine."

Mom unhooked the phone and unstrapped the monitor. "Do you want to say hello to your baby sister or brother?"

"You mean call it on the phone?" I asked.

Mom shook her head. "No, you can talk to it directly."

"Hi, lazybones," I said, putting my hand on Mom's belly. The skin there felt stretched tight, not like the skin around a muscle, but almost translucent and very smooth. Something bumped against my hand.

"She's doing a roundoff, I think," said Mom.

"She's probably doing it better than I am," I said.

"How was gym today?" asked Mom. "I hope you weren't too upset by what happened to me."

"No," I said. "I was actually having a great day until we got to the beam. I'm still having trouble with the new roundoff somersault dismount that Patrick wants us to do. Now he made us try it on the real beam."

"And how did it go?" Mom asked.

"It didn't," I said. "I was really cooking, but then when I got on the beam, I just couldn't do it."

"It's a difficult dismount," said Mom.

"Yeah, but the other Pinecones did it. Not great, but they did it. I just couldn't do it," I said.

"You'll get it," said Mom.

Barney and Nick came back in the room. Barney was carrying a tray with herb tea on it. I wanted to talk to Mom some more about what happened to me on the beam, but not in front of Nick.

I got up so Barney could put the tray down.

"The baby and I could get used to this kind of service," said Mom jokingly.

Nick looked at me. "I know what it's going to be," he said.

"You mean, you know if it's a boy or a girl?" I exclaimed. "How did you find out?" It would make me really mad if Barney had told Nick and kept me in the dark.

"It doesn't matter," said Nick. "It's going to be born spoiled. Two months in bed — who wouldn't be spoiled?"

"Nick," said Mom, "I promise you this baby won't be spoiled."

50

Nick was looking very uncomfortable. He and I were just getting used to each other, and now we had to get ready for another brother or sister. Just what Nick and I needed — a born-spoiled sibling. It just wasn't fair.

Use Your Head

It's amazing what you can get used to. One minute you have a normal mother — all right, she wasn't everybody's idea of a normal mom — not everybody's mom can do a double back flip. Still, I thought of her as normal. All my life she has always worked in a gym, first hers and Dad's in St. Louis, and then as a coach at Patrick's.

Now, suddenly, she was this person with a big belly who lay in bed all day. It wasn't quite as awful as it must sound. First of all, she didn't act sick. She had a lot of energy.

She talked on the telephone a lot. Nick might be worried that the new baby would be spoiled. I was worried that it would be born with a miniature telephone in its ear.

Barney got her a laptop computer, and Mom worked on it all the time. She was computerizing all of Patrick's records.

We ate better than ever. Barney had set up a card table in the bedroom, and we all took our dinners with Mom. Mom joked that we might as well have moved into a one-room apartment rather than a big new house, but it really wasn't so bad.

I usually stopped home after school before I went to the gym to see if Mom needed anything. She had only a little time to go before the baby was due.

"Anything I can do for you today?" I asked.

"Nope," she said. "I'm doing fine. I've got a surprise for you at the gym."

"Excuse me?" I said. "You haven't been to the gym, have you?"

Mom smiled. "No, this bed doesn't have wheels, though I wouldn't mind that. I faxed something over to Patrick that I think will help you."

"Are you going to name the baby 'Fax'?" I asked her.

"I was thinking more of calling him or her 'Modem.'"

"So what's my surprise that I'm going to find at the gym?" I asked.

"If I told you, it would ruin the surprise," said

Mom. "Get going. I'm fine. Barney will be home soon."

"Are you really okay?" I asked her.

Mom nodded. I took off for the gym.

"How's your mom?" Patrick asked me as soon as I showed up at the gym.

"You mean you didn't talk to her today?" I asked. "She said she faxed you a surprise for me."

"Our computer records have never been so up-to-date. She's got a list of every trick for every gymnast in the gym."

I made a face. "I guess she left a lot of blanks for me on the beam, huh? What's the surprise?"

"Just go change into your leotard, and then I'll show you. It should help. You're just going through a rough patch with the beam, Jodi. We're going to practice on it today."

"Great," I groaned. "What a wonderful surprise!"

I went into the locker room to change. "How's your mom?" Lauren asked.

"Fine," I said with a sigh.

"What's wrong?" Lauren asked.

"Beam today," I groaned.

"Oh, no," said Becky. "Don't tell me. We're going to be treated to another episode of Jodi frozen on the beam."

"Give it a rest, Becky," said Lauren. "Jodi's just having a tough time with that one trick. It can happen to anybody."

"That's true," said Heidi. "I remember when it happened to Nadia Malinovich, the great Russian gymnast. It was at the worlds last year. She fell off during the compulsories on the beam routine, and from then on she couldn't do anything right on the beam."

"Thanks, Heidi," I said sarcastically.

"I was just saying that if it can happen to a world-class gymnast like Nadia Malinovich, it can happen to you. By the way, how's your mom?"

I was getting a little bit tired of "How's your mom?" as a topic of conversation.

"She's fine," I said.

I grabbed my gym shoes and headed out for the gym.

Cindi, Darlene, Ti An, and Ashley were already warming up. "How's your mom?" Darlene asked me.

"I'm thinking of having a T-shirt made up that says 'She's fine,' " I snapped.

"Sorry," said Darlene. "I just wanted to know."

"She *is* fine," I said. "I didn't mean to snap. It's just that Patrick said we'd be working on the beam today. You know how I've been on the beam lately."

"Oh, you'll get it," said Darlene.

"Easy for you to say. Beam is your best event," I muttered as we completed our stretches.

Patrick came up to us with a stack of computer printouts in his hand. "Girls," he said. "I want all the intermediates and advanced gymnasts to look at what I have here."

"Oh, no, just my luck," I muttered. "Becky and her gang will be working with us today."

"You'll show them," said Darlene.

Becky's group, the Needles, gathered around the beam. "What do you want, Patrick?" Becky asked.

"I'd like you all to study these computer drawings," he said.

"Uh-oh, the latest from my mom?" I asked.

Patrick nodded. "She's made computer drawings of the move that you've been having trouble with — the roundoff back-somersault dismount," he said. "It shows the biomechanics of it. I made copies for everybody."

Patrick handed out the papers. It showed a little stick figure on the beam moving through the roundoff and into the somersault.

"It *always* looks easy on paper," I complained. "A computer gymnast can do anything."

"A computer gymnast can't do *anything* on a real beam," said Patrick. "Still, your mom thinks she might have spotted your problem."

56

"From her bed?" I said. "Mom hasn't seen me work out for months. And please don't tell me it has anything to do with Mom being pregnant."

Patrick gave me a strange look. "I never thought that. I think it's a mechanical problem, and your mom's computer drawings helped me figure it out. Actually it's a very common problem, even among advanced gymnasts."

"Let me see that drawing," said Heidi.

Mom had shown the stick figure doing the move in two different ways.

"Try to figure out the difference between the two drawings," said Patrick.

"I see the problem," said Heidi after looking at it for about two seconds.

Patrick smiled. "Heidi, don't say anything. Let the others figure it out for themselves."

I studied the drawings. The two different figures didn't look very different from each other.

"Use your head," Heidi whispered to me.

I looked at the picture again. One of the figures had lifted its head when it was upside down in the roundoff.

"The head?" I asked Patrick.

Patrick beamed at me as if I had just gotten an A+.

"That's using your old noggin," said Patrick, tapping his forehead with his finger. "You're exactly right. You've been lifting your head when you're upside down in the roundoff. You can see that when the figure does that, it throws the alignment off, and that's why you've been falling off the beam. Now that you know what you've been doing wrong, we can fix it."

"Right," I said. But I had my doubts.

10

Take a Break

"No fair," complained Becky. "Heidi helped her."

"I did not," Heidi protested.

Patrick shushed Becky. "This isn't a test," he said. "Jodi, come on up here and let's see if we can get it right in real life."

"This isn't fair," I complained. "I get the right answer and that means I've got to be first."

"Come on, Jodi," said Patrick. I hopped up without complaining and stood on the beam. I wasn't going to give in to this feeling of dread.

The beam was the same height it had always been. I looked down to the end.

Patrick stood by my side, chatting to me. "When you're doing a roundoff before a dismount on the beam, it's natural to want to see the take-off point. So you've been lifting your head to see the end of the beam, but that causes your back to arch, and you go sideways and then you're slowing your roundoff. . . ."

Patrick's voice droned on. I nodded my head. Patrick looked up at me. "Jodi, stop nodding your head with every word." He patted me on the leg.

"Okay, let's try it again. I want you to cheat a little on the pirouette. That will give you a chance to see the end of the beam sooner, but concentrate on keeping your head down."

"Yes, Patrick."

"Picture the movement in your head."

"I am," I promised him. I was trying to, but my heart had started pounding again, and my hands were perspiring. I licked my lips.

"Okay," said Patrick. "Let's try it for real."

I pushed up onto the beam. I willed myself not to be afraid.

I took one step on the beam, and I fell off.

"Whoops," I said, embarrassed. "I guess I lifted my head."

I picked myself off the mat and got right back on the beam. I didn't want Patrick to think I was chicken.

Patrick just smiled at me. "Okay, let's try

again." I lifted my leg to start the roundoff, and I fell off the beam again.

I could hear somebody titter. I knew it was probably Becky.

"It's okay, Jodi. Maybe you're getting all your falling over *before* the trick. You'll get over the jitters and do it fine," said Patrick.

"In this century or the next?" asked Becky.

"Becky," warned Patrick. "I invited the Needles over to work with the Pinecones because I thought the computer printout would be valuable for all of you. I didn't invite you to 'needle' Jodi."

I had turned bright red. "Patrick," I said, "maybe you should get somebody else to do this first."

"No, come on, Jodi. Hop back on."

I sighed. I obediently got back on the beam.

I willed myself not to fall off. "Don't fall off, don't fall off," I repeated to myself as if it were a prayer.

Patrick saw my lips moving. "What are you saying?" he asked.

"I'm telling myself not to fall off," I admitted.

"Concentrate on completing the trick; don't think about falling."

"Trying *not* to fall off is the best way *to* fall off," said Heidi.

"Thank you very much for those words of wisdom," I said sarcastically.

"It's true," said Patrick.

He was starting to get impatient. "Jodi, you know darned well the beam isn't going anywhere. Just go for it."

I took a deep breath and lifted my leg to do the roundoff.

I fell off even before I could begin.

"Jodi, tell me specifically what you're afraid of," Patrick asked.

"I'm afraid of falling on my head," I said.

Becky giggled.

Patrick glared at her. He got a mat and draped it over the edge of the beam.

"I want you to practice falling," he said.

"I think I've been doing that," I said.

"No, really practice. Dive for the beam, head-first, but remember to cradle your head with your arms."

I looked at Patrick as if he were crazy.

"Go on," he said. "Try it."

I dived headfirst onto the beam, protecting my head with my arms and falling off to the side.

I did it twice. Then finally Patrick sent me to the back of the line.

I watched as my teammates all tried the dismount. Lauren fell the first time doing the roundoff, but the second time she did it. She landed on her knees after the somersault, but she did it.

Darlene couldn't get enough height on the somersault to get around. Patrick had to hold her up, but still, on the next try, she went all the way around.

Ashley did it the first time she tried it. She squealed with pleasure. "I don't believe I did it!" she yelled. Then she saw the dirty look I gave her and she shut up.

Cindi completed it on her second try, and, like Ashley, Ti An didn't even need two tries. I could tell this was going to be a spectacular dismount for her.

Patrick looked around at the Pinecones. I was kind of half-hiding behind Lauren.

"Jodi?" he asked.

"I'm really exhausted," I said.

"Try it," said Patrick.

I shook my head. "Honest, Patrick, I think I'm too tired. I'm scared I'll hurt myself."

Patrick's eyes narrowed. Then he nodded his head. "Okay, Jodi," he said. "Maybe you've had enough for today."

I wondered if the United States Gymnastics Federation could invent a special category for gymnasts who suddenly turned chicken.

"I changed my mind. I'll try the trick again," I said to Patrick determinedly. I knew that Patrick always admired gymnasts who didn't quit.

Patrick shook his head. "You can take a break from it today," he said.

I should have been happy, but I wasn't. In fact, I felt lousy.

I Think I Created
a Monster

Nick was outside our house when I came back from practice. He had his skateboard out, but he wasn't playing with it. He was just sitting with it on the front steps.

"Out of my way, squirt," I said.

"I didn't do anything wrong," Nick said. He moved out of my way quickly, in a very un-Nick-like manner. He was right. He hadn't done anything wrong. I shouldn't have picked on him.

"Sorry," I said.

Nick looked at me in surprise. He wasn't used to me saying "I'm sorry." He sighed.

"What's wrong with you?" I asked.

"I'm never gonna learn to skateboard," he said. "I'm too scared. Every time the thing gathers up speed I want to jump off."

"If you're scared, you're scared, and there's nothing you can do about it," I said.

"I wish I were more like you," said Nick. "You're never scared of anything."

"Ha! You should have seen me on the beam," I said. I took the skateboard from Nick and started easily sailing up and down the sidewalk. I took it slow. I flipped the skateboard up and stepped off it.

"You do it," I said. "Take it real slow."

"But I'm too scared of it," whined Nick. He sounded a lot like me, trembling on the end of the beam, only I never said the words, "I'm too scared."

"Time to fish or cut bait," I teased him.

"I don't know what that means," he said.

"I don't, either," I admitted. Nick took the skateboard from me. He worked up a little momentum and then he hopped off.

"Why did you do that?" I asked him.

"I'm waiting till I don't feel scared," he said. "Don't yell at me."

"I'm the last person to yell at you," I said. "Nick, if you don't want to do it, you don't have to."

I could tell he wanted me to tell him that he *had* to get on the skateboard and just do it.

"How's Mom today?" I asked him.

"She's getting as big as the house," Nick said.

"It won't be long now," I said. "What do you want — a baby sister or brother?"

"Brother," said Nick without hesitating.

"Thanks a heap," I said. I started to go inside.

"Jodi?" asked Nick.

"What?" I asked.

"Will you run alongside me while I try it again?" Nick was usually such a bossy little kid, it was strange to have him ask nicely.

"Sure," I said.

I put my hand on the small of his back, just to steady him, the way that Patrick would do for me. I didn't have to run very fast, because Nick was too timid to get up much speed. I ran alongside him.

Without warning, even though we weren't going very fast, Nick stepped off the skateboard. The board flipped up and hit me in the chest.

"Ouch!" I yelled at him. "Why didn't you give me warning?"

Nick was breathing hard. "I couldn't help myself," he said. "I just got scared."

"Oh, cut that out," I shouted. I knew that I shouldn't have lost my temper with him, but he was making me mad. "Either do it or don't."

Nick looked like he was going to cry. His face got all red and splotchy.

"You don't even care if I'm scared," he whined.

"You're the one who wants to skateboard," I said to him. "I'm not making you."

Nick's face got redder. He took the skateboard from me and plopped it down on the ground. He put his left foot on it, and then he pushed off. He got his balance, and he was sailing. He even managed to make it curve a tiny bit.

He hopped off and turned to me. I think he expected me to still be mad at him.

I wasn't. I grinned at him. "Way to go, Nick. You really got the rhythm of it."

"I did, didn't I?" he bragged. "I'm probably going to be better than you at this."

I stared at him. "What do you mean?" I growled.

"I'm a boy," he said. "Boys are better skateboarders. Everybody knows that."

I stuck my tongue out at him. "You . . . you . . ." I sputtered. "You were scared of a tiny crack in the sidewalk before I helped you."

"I'm not anymore," bragged Nick. He pushed off again. I stared at his back. I had created a monster. Then I thought about the possibility of having another baby brother. Two monsters! It was too much.

Let's Make a Deal

Two weeks later, Mom was still getting bigger, and I was still falling off the beam. It was just ridiculous.

Everything else was going fine for me.

"I might as well not show up on beam day," I groaned to Darlene in the locker room.

"It's just a phase," she said.

Becky began to make clucking noises.

"Becky, shut up," said Heidi. "This is very traumatic for Jodi."

I wanted to laugh. I really didn't feel that traumatized. I mean, I'd be scared if I had lost my nerve on the vault or on the bars, but I hadn't. It was just the stupid beam.

"The guy who invented the beam had to be an

idiot!" I said. "I should have been born a boy. Boys don't have to go on the beam."

"Then you'd have to do the rings," said Ti An seriously. "I don't like the rings."

"It's not like I have a choice, do I?" I said.

"I guess not," said Cindi.

We went out into the gym. I thought about my words "I don't have a choice." They weren't really true. Patrick couldn't hold a gun to my head to make me do tricks on the beam. We finished our warm-ups.

Becky and the advanced group were working over the pits. Maybe I just needed more time in the pits.

Patrick was a reasonable man. He just didn't like surprises. Most coaches don't.

Patrick was adjusting the uneven bars. He smiled at me. Patrick's got a great smile.

"Hi, Jodi. How's your mom?" he asked.

"She's getting so big that she says she'd have trouble getting out of bed, even if they let her," I said.

"I bet you'll be as glad as she is when this is all over," he said.

"Right." I really didn't want to talk about Mom.

"Patrick," I said. I knew Patrick liked directness. "I've been thinking about my dismount. Maybe I just need more practice in the pit. If I could get where I feel sure of it. . . ."

70

Patrick held up his hand. "No," he said simply.

"No?" I repeated. I couldn't believe it. He just said a flat "no." "What do you mean, no?"

"You heard me," said Patrick. "You're not doing it in the pits again. You've done it dozens of times into the pit. I know you hurt yourself doing this move, but that was months ago. I've been patient with you. We've broken it down into its components. Your mom even made that computer printout for you. You know the mechanics of it. You just have to do it. And the judges don't care how well you do it into the foam pit. If you can't do it up on the beam, it's worth nothing to you at all."

"But I *can't* do it! You've seen that."

Patrick looked impatient. "Then we'll just have to stop wasting time with it," he said.

I put my hands on my hips. "What does that mean?" I asked.

"Jodi, it's your choice. I can't hold a gun to your head."

I grinned at him. "That's exactly what I thought . . . that's why I knew you'd let me practice it a little longer in the pit."

"No!" said Patrick, a little more sharply. "You'll either do it on the regulation beam, or you won't do it. We'll kiss that trick good-bye."

"You'd let me just quit on it?" I said.

"Sometimes you just have to let it go," said

Patrick. I had the feeling that he was giving up on me.

"But I never give up," I said. "It's just this one trick. It's got me paralyzed. But I'll get over it. I need more time."

"How much time?" Patrick asked.

"I don't know," I said impatiently. "How would I know how long it's going to take?"

"You tell me," said Patrick. "Give me a date, and either you do it by then or we forget about it."

"I can't do that," I whined.

Patrick tapped his foot impatiently. "Jodi, I'm not doing this to punish you, but we're not going to waste any more time on this dismount. It's getting to be too big an obstacle in your way. It's time to either do it or forget about it."

"Okay, okay," I said. "I'll do it by the end of the week. But I think you're being unfair."

"I'm serious about this," said Patrick. "We have a deal. Either you do the roundoff somie dismount by the end of the week, or we forget about it for six months. This isn't punishment."

"Yeah, yeah," I muttered. "I heard you."

I went back to the Pinecones who had gathered around the regulation beam.

"What was that all about?" asked Lauren.

"Patrick's fed up with me," I said.

"What does that mean?" Lauren asked.

"He's convinced that I'm never going to do the stupid dismount," I said. "He doesn't want me to try anymore."

Darlene was the one who saw through me. "Jodi," she said. "Exactly what did Patrick say."

I sighed.

"Well?" asked Darlene.

"He says that I have to do the trick by the end of the week, or I can't even try it again for six months."

Heidi nodded. "Oh, yeah, the now or never ploy," she said. "I've had coaches try it on me before."

"What do you mean?" I asked.

"It's just Patrick's way of making you do the trick," said Heidi. "I think it's smart. You've got yourself blocked about it. I've seen it happen before. A kid takes a particular skill right to the brink and then they go berserk."

"Thanks, Heidi. I *love* being called crazy."

"Nobody's calling you crazy. It's just that you shouldn't analyze yourself to bits. Just do it."

"Easy for you to say, Heidi. You can do a round-off double-back. And you're never scared."

"Wrong," said Heidi. "I get scared. I don't take stupid risks, and I just don't waste energy on being scared. You're wasting too much energy on this trick. That's your problem."

"Thanks," I said.

"I mean it," said Heidi. I knew she was trying to help. The problem was everybody was trying to help me. All the help in the world wasn't going to stop me from falling.

You Never Stop Being Afraid

"Jodi, is that you?" Mom had a megaphone on her bed. She called out to me from the bedroom.

I went into her room. If I had kept *my* room in such a mess, Mom would have killed me. There were stacks of books and papers everywhere and bottles of juice. The monitor and its straps were lying on the bed table. The telephone was in the middle of the bed.

"Do you need anything?" I asked her.

"Yes," said Mom. "A kiss."

I kissed her on the cheek and patted her belly for good luck. "Hi, there, little sister," I said.

"Are you hoping for a girl?" Mom asked.

I nodded. "Nick is one brother too many," I said.

Mom grinned at me. "You've been terrific with

him, honey," she said. "Barney was worried that it was going to be a lot tougher for the two of you to get along."

I shrugged. I didn't deserve much credit. Nick was still a pest as far as I was concerned. It was just that now he was *my* pest.

Mom sat up in bed.

"I had a lousy time in gym today," I said.

"What's bothering you, Jodi?" she asked.

"It's nothing," I said.

"Come on, Jodi," said Mom. "I might be stuck in bed, but I'm not sick, and can still see things. You're feeling blue. It's not like you to be down. You and I, we get down and then we get mad and then we do something about it!"

"I'm not feeling blue," I lied.

"So what is it?"

I played with the satin trimming on Mom's blanket. When I was little I used to wear out the trimmings on my blankets by rubbing them with my fingers. "I'm chicken."

Mom sat up straighter in bed. "Becky!" she said angrily. "I'll strangle the girl. Somebody's got to talk to her." Mom's temper is even scarier than mine.

"Mom, cool it," I said. "It's not Becky this time. I admit it is true that she clucks like a chicken when I walk past these days."

"That's inexcusable," exclaimed Mom. "I'll talk to Patrick."

"Mom, Becky's not the problem," I said. "Patrick thinks I'm chicken, too."

Mom's eyes narrowed. She looked like she was spitting fire.

"Patrick does *not* think you're chicken," she said. "Where did you get this idea? Becky must have been the one to poison you about Patrick."

"Mom, Becky hasn't said a word to me about Patrick. This isn't a Becky problem, believe me."

"Then what is it?" Mom asked.

"It's me. It's been months now that Patrick's been trying to teach me the roundoff somie dismount. All the other Pinecones are doing it. I get up on the beam, and I'm paralyzed."

"Are you keeping your head down during the roundoff?" asked Mom. "If you lift your head, it throws you sideways. . . . Here, I can show you." Mom reached for the computer.

I put my hand over hers. "Mom, it's not a technical problem. I understand that. I've seen all the little computer drawings you've made on how to do it. It's me. I never used to be scared, and now every time I'm on the beam, I'm afraid I won't land on my feet."

Mom nodded. "You're trying to get *off* the beam, not stay on. You're anticipating a fall."

I nodded. "Every time I get on the beam, I *know* I'm going to fall. And it didn't used to be like that. I mean, I was never the best person on the beam, but I wasn't scared of it. I didn't used to be scared of anything."

"You weren't always the greatest gymnast, either," said Mom softly. "You weren't nearly as good as you could be."

"Thanks a bunch for that confidence-raiser, Mom," I said sarcastically. "I'll always come to you with my problems." I started to pull away and stand up. Mom grabbed my hand.

"Jodi, stay," she said. "I can't run after you. Stay and talk to me. You misunderstood me."

"I heard you fine, Mom. You said I'm not a great gymnast. I always knew I was a disappointment to you and Dad. It's probably why you got divorced."

As soon as the words were out of my mouth, I knew that I didn't really mean them. I was just feeling sorry for myself.

"Jodi, come off it," said Mom. Even nearly nine months pregnant and after being in bed for a couple of months, my mom is very hard to con.

I still felt sorry for myself. "You said I wasn't a great gymnast. You don't have to remind me of how many trophies you won when you were my age."

"And yet, I was afraid a lot of the time," said Mom.

"*You* were!" I've seen old films of Mom doing gymnastics. "You were almost as good as Heidi is now. You looked totally fearless."

"The number-one factor separating good gymnasts from great ones is how they cope with fear," said Mom. "Nobody gets away with no fear."

"But I didn't used to be afraid, and you just said that I wasn't great."

"That's right," said Mom. "A total lack of fear is not a healthy sign. I always knew that when you stopped being such a daredevil, you'd really develop your potential."

"Oh, no, the dreaded *p* word," I groaned. Mom knows how much I hate being told that I have potential. I've been told that all my life.

"Laugh, but I'm being serious," said Mom. "Some people think that daring gymnasts are born — you either have guts or you don't," said Mom. "It's not true. To be truly great, you've got to learn to control your fear."

"Thanks, Mom. You haven't told me how."

"No one can tell you, Jodi," said Mom. "It's something each of us has to learn ourselves. And we never stop."

"Never stop being afraid?" I asked.

"Never stop learning how to deal with it," said Mom, picking at the blanket on her bed.

"Are you scared about having this baby?" I asked Mom.

Mom smiled. "Jodi, nobody ever said you were dumb."

"Actually, Mom, that's not true," I reminded her. "Plenty of my teachers have hinted it. They might not have really said it, but — "

"Jodi," said Mom, "you know you're not stupid. Actually, though, I'm not scared about having the baby. I just want to be sure that the baby's okay. I'll be very happy when I finally give birth, but there's nothing I can do but wait."

"Patrick won't let me wait," I said. "He says that I have to do the trick by the end of the week, or I've got to forget it."

"Sounds like good advice," said Mom.

"I was afraid you'd say that," I said. "Don't you have any other suggestions?"

"You could let me give you a hug," said Mom.

"Is that supposed to give me courage?" I teased her.

"No," said Mom. "But it'll make me feel better." Mom and I hugged. I could barely get my arms around her.

"I'll be glad when you're normal size again," I said.

"So will I," said Mom. "So will I."

Starting to Grow Up

Patrick took me aside before I had a chance to change in the locker room. "Today is Friday," he said.

"Thanks. I knew that. I don't exactly have to be reminded," I snapped. "I didn't have to write the date down in my calendar. I know. It's the day that I either do the trick or don't."

"Jodi, don't get mad at me," warned Patrick. "I wondered if maybe you didn't want an audience. We could find a time that nobody else is here."

I stared at Patrick. "You'd clear the whole gym out for me?" I asked him.

"I want this to be as easy for you as possible,"

said Patrick. "I know it's been hard on you, these past few months."

"You mean all that falling off the beam?" I asked.

Patrick shook his head. "No," he said. "I meant having so much to deal with, your mom's pregnancy, the fact that you're scared for her."

"That's *not* why I've been falling off the beam," I protested. I was furious.

"I know," said Patrick. "I just wanted you to know that if you wanted me to clear the gym, I'd be willing to do it."

"No, thanks," I said. I wasn't sure why that idea made me so angry, but it did.

I stomped off to the locker room. "I dare anybody to remind me that today is Friday," I said.

"Today is Friday," said Cindi. "You know I can't resist a dare."

I blinked. Cindi laughed. "Well," she protested. "I said it. Are you going to punch me out?"

"No," I said. "I'm just so mad. Patrick offered to clear the gym when it's time for me to do the trick. I don't know how I got myself into this. It's really not fair."

"What's not fair?" asked Ti An.

"That Patrick won't let me practice the round-off somie in the pit anymore. He says I either do it on the beam, or else forget it for six months."

"I'd like to forget it," said Ti An. "That trick

scares me every time I do it. I'm terrified of it."

"Ti An," I said, "you always say you're afraid and then, at the last moment, you do it fine."

Ti An giggled, as if I had just found out a secret about her.

"Don't worry," I whispered. "I won't tell anybody. You can keep on saying you're scared."

Heidi came into the locker room. "Hey, Jodi, I've been looking for you."

"Oh, great," I mumbled.

"I wanted to wish you good luck," said Heidi. "I was thinking about you today. You can't get too psychological. You can't wait for fear to go away. The only time to master it is now."

"Thanks for the pep talk, Heidi," I said. I sighed.

Heidi looked at me. "I guess you've been getting lots of good advice lately, huh?"

I nodded.

"It doesn't do much good, does it?" she said.

"It can't hurt," I said. I put on my bright red leotard. If mom could wear bright red, so could I.

"Is that your lucky leotard?" Heidi asked.

"I'm not sure I've *got* a lucky leotard," I said. "I'm not sure that this has got anything to do with luck."

Darlene came late into the locker room. She patted me on the back so hard that I practically fell over. "Good luck today," she said.

Heidi started laughing. It wasn't like Heidi to laugh out loud.

"What did I say that was so funny?" Darlene insisted.

"Jodi's face," said Heidi. "She looks like she's facing the electric chair."

"Thanks a lot," I said. "Maybe I should take Patrick up on his offer to clear the gym."

"You wouldn't want to do that," said Lauren. "It's a proven fact that a Pinecone needs the other Pinecones around."

"Lauren, you're making that up. That's not a proven fact," I said.

"Well, not scientifically proven," said Lauren. "But I *know* that it's true."

"What is true?" askled Becky.

"That the Pinecones need other Pinecones," said Lauren.

Becky rolled her eyes. "Would you give me a break? All the world's top gymnasts are individualists. Isn't that true, Heidi?"

"It's a proven fact," said Heidi, "that the best gymnasts need each other."

"Oh, no," said Becky. "It's catching."

"What's that?" asked Heidi.

"Pinecone fever — it's affected your brain," she said. "It's like fear . . . it's catching." Becky looked at me.

"Becky, I'm not ashamed to say that I'm

scared," I said. "I've been lousing up the same trick for months. It would be stupid to say that I'm not afraid."

Heidi was staring at me. "What are you staring at?" I asked her.

"I think you just grew up," she said.

15

Prove It

I was very careful doing my warm-ups. I flexed my fingers and wrists and then my ankles. I rolled my head around my neck, and then I started my slow stretches.

Patrick came up to me. He watched me carefully.

"Are you ready?" he asked.

"What?" I exclaimed. "NO! I haven't done my sit-ups or shoulder stretches. I'm not ready at all."

"Okay," said Patrick. "I'll wait."

"I don't get it," I complained as I laid on my back and grabbed the edges of the mat to stretch out my shoulder blades.

"Get what?" asked Patrick. He was standing

over my head, and from this angle he looked huge.

"Why do I have to do it right away?" I asked. "We could do it at the end of the session. You said that I had to do it today. You didn't say it had to be the first thing. It's making too big a deal out of it."

I sat up and flipped around so that I was facing Patrick. He had his arms crossed over his chest.

"I don't want to wait all through the session. It'll be on your mind," he said. "It'll be on the other Pinecones' minds, and it'll be on my mind."

"Well, you're the one who said we had to set the silly date to begin with," I argued. "I'd be willing to still practice a little more, sneak up on the little sucker gradually."

At least I got half a smile out of Patrick. "Jodi, we've been sneaking up on this trick for months. A deal's a deal."

"Yeah, yeah," I said.

"You can't go back on a deal," said Lauren, teasingly.

"Thank you very much, Lauren," I said. "I needed that little lesson on morality."

Before Lauren could retort, Patrick raised his hand. "Girls," he said, "this is between Jodi and me. It's Jodi's choice that the other Pinecones can watch. And Lauren, it is *not* a big deal. Jodi has been doing beautifully on the other apparatus these past few months. All it means is that we're going to put aside this particular dismount off the beam. It's nothing else."

"Wait a minute," I complained. "You're assuming that I'm *not* going to do it."

"I'm not assuming anything, Jodi," said Patrick. He held his hand out to me to help me off the mats.

"You *want* me to fall," I whined.

Patrick stopped. I looked up at him. I knew that wasn't true. Of all people, Patrick didn't want me to fall.

"You know that's not true," he said softly.

I nodded.

"You can't wait to do something just because you're waiting for the fear to go away. It doesn't work that way," he said. "You've got all the technique and skills to do this trick. You can do it."

"I'm not sure that I can," I said.

Patrick looked impatient again. "Jodi, we have a deal. But if you want to put it off, I understand. Maybe if we just waited until a few months after the baby is born."

"Gimme a break," I shouted a little louder than I intended. "This doesn't have to do with Mom. This doesn't have to do with having a new baby. I don't know why I'm scared, but this is for real. Every time I've tried this trick, I've fallen hard. I've turned black and blue twice. I'm not scared just because I'm having a little sister or brother. Everybody is making a case for it. This is about me!"

Patrick was about to say something, but I wouldn't let him. I just exploded. "All anybody talks about is my mom having a baby and having to stay in bed. I swear to you, this isn't about that. It's me. It's me!"

"Fine, Jodi," said Patrick. "Prove it."

16

When Does It Ever Stop?

I looked longingly over at the pit.

Patrick followed my eyes and shook his head subtly.

"No fair reading my mind," I said. I chewed on my lower lip.

Patrick patted the beam. "Take a second," he suggested. "Think about the movement. Picture it. Break it down into its parts. Do you have any questions about it?"

I saw myself doing the roundoff. I saw myself falling right on my head.

"Stop!" I said to myself. I thought I said it to myself, but I must have spoken out loud.

"Stop what?" asked Patrick.

"I was saying it to myself," I said. "I was starting to picture myself falling on my head again."

"It never happened, Jodi," said Patrick. "You fell on your side and into the pit."

"That's right, isn't it?" I said.

"Is there anything else you want to go over?" Patrick asked me.

I saw myself finishing the roundoff and landing solidly on the beam, and then pushing off into the back somersault, throwing my hands into the air, getting enough distance from the end of the beam, rotating safely in the air, and landing as lightly as Sar-Cat.

I opened my eyes.

"Ready?" asked Patrick.

I wasn't. I was scared, but there was nothing I could do about the fear.

I climbed onto the beam. I shook my hands, trying to release the tension, but it wouldn't go away. I had been nervous before in competitions, but that kind of tension was almost a high. It made me feel sharp. Today I didn't feel sharp; I felt clammy.

I looked at the end of the beam. Then I raised my hands over my head and jumped. My hands hit the beam and rebounded back up. This was the moment that both my hands and feet were off the beam. I twisted in the air, and my feet landed on the beam, one behind the other.

Now, with my back to the end of the beam, I used my momentum to push off the beam again. This time I was flying high in the air, but I was rotating off to the side. I could see that I was too close to the end of the beam. I had to pull out of the somersault. I cradled my head with my arms and fell onto the mats on my side.

I was breathing hard. I looked up at Patrick. I wasn't hurt. I had come so close.

Patrick patted me on the back.

"I fell on the landing," I said. "I overrotated coming off the roundoff."

Patrick was grinning.

"What are you smiling about?" I asked him.

"I never said you had to do it perfectly," said Patrick. "You're over the hump. You did it."

"I did?" I asked incredulously.

I looked over at the Pinecones. Darlene, Lauren, Cindi, Ti An, and even Ashley were punching their fists into the air.

"All right!" I exploded. I ran over to them, punching the air with my fist. "All right!" I repeated.

"Way to go, Jodi," said Heidi.

"I fell on the landing," I said.

"It doesn't matter," said Heidi. "You didn't freeze. You'll be able to clean it up."

"Thanks," I said. "You helped me."

"I did?" Heidi said. She sounded surprised.

I nodded. "All along, you kept telling me that fear was natural."

"It is," said Heidi. "It's taken me a long time to realize that. I used to be like you. I used to think that I had to be fearless."

Patrick came up to us. "Girls, I'd like to speak to Jodi alone for a minute."

The Pinecones and Heidi left us. I looked up at Patrick. "I'm proud of you, Jodi," he said.

"I know," I said impatiently. "I conquered my fear and all that."

Patrick shook his head. "That's not what I meant."

I stared at him. "Then what did you mean? I showed you I could do it. I was really mad at you for making me set the date, but now I'm glad."

"I wanted you to be mad at me," said Patrick. "It helped you forget about being afraid. I'm proud of you for getting mad enough at me to do it."

I blushed. "I used the same technique on Nick," I admitted. "And it worked."

"Of course, now you've got to do it all over again," said Patrick.

I groaned. "When does it ever stop?" I asked him.

"It doesn't. That's the best thing about gymnastics" — Patrick paused. He grinned at me — "and life. If you're lucky, you never stop finding new challenges."

I guess I'm lucky.

17

I'm Your Big Sister

I'd just gotten to the gym after school when suddenly Becky burst into the locker room. "Jodi!" she yelled.

"What?" I yelled back. I figured Becky was looking for something new to put me down about — now that she could no longer pick on me for falling off the beam.

"Patrick wants you," she said.

"Now what?" I asked.

"I don't know," said Becky, sounding annoyed. "Maybe he's had second thoughts about telling you how wonderful you were for doing that stupid trick last week."

"Thanks, Becky. You're a big help."

"I am?" asked Becky, sounding surprised.

"Yeah," I said. "I love to prove you wrong. It's a great incentive."

I walked out of the locker room to see what Patrick wanted.

"It's your mom," he said. "She's having the baby. Barney called me and asked if I would take you to the hospital. We'll pick up Nick at his gym."

"Is she okay?" I yelled.

The Pinecones heard me and came running out of the locker room. "What's wrong?" Cindi asked.

"My mom," I said. "She's having the baby."

"I think everything's just fine," said Patrick.

"Think?" I repeated. "You don't *know*?"

"Jodi, we'll be at the hospital in just a few minutes," said Patrick.

"Good luck," said Darlene.

"I'll come back to the gym as soon as I've dropped Jodi off," Patrick said to the Pinecones. "Do your warm-ups. Gerald will watch over things."

Patrick stopped at the Atomic Amazons' gym to pick up Nick. I waited in the car. Nick looked kind of pale when he walked back with Patrick.

"I thought it wasn't supposed to be till next week," Nick said as he climbed into the backseat.

"I guess our baby brother or sister got tired of lying in bed," I said. My voice sounded funny to me, as if I were saying words, but the words weren't connected to me.

I stared out the window. I was as nervous as Nick.

Patrick parked the car. We had to wait at the information desk while Patrick got directions to the maternity ward. Everybody getting off the elevator was carrying flowers or helium balloons.

"This way," said Patrick. He guided us down the hall and then pointed to an open door.

He started to turn back toward the waiting room. "Aren't you coming in?" I asked him.

"I'll wait out here," said Patrick. "This is just for family."

Nick grabbed my hand. It was funny to think that Nick was family, but I guess it was true.

We started to walk into Mom's room. A nurse stopped us. "Are you part of the immediate Josephson family?" she asked.

Nick and I looked at each other. "I guess we are related," I said.

The nurse smiled at us. "You must be Nick and Jodi," she said. "Your mom and dad said you'd be here. Just scrub your hands and put on a hospital gown."

Nick and I did as we were told. The hospital gown was way too big for Nick. It looked very silly.

We walked into Mom's room. Barney was sitting next to Mom's bed. She looked pretty good, but she still looked kind of big. I figured we had gotten there in time. She hadn't had the baby.

Barney grinned. I ran to her bed and hugged her. "Are you okay?" I asked.

"I'm fine," said Mom. "Just fine." She gave Nick a kiss. Nick looked shy and uncomfortable.

"Well, kids," said Mom. "Don't you want to meet your new brother?"

"Oh, no, Mom, you didn't," I blurted out. "You didn't have it already?"

Mom nodded. "I couldn't wait."

"And it's a boy!" exclaimed Barney.

Mom smiled. I guess with two girls of her own, Mom was entitled to want a boy.

"Come on," said Barney. "I want to introduce you to Travis Josephson."

I hadn't noticed, but in the corner of the room was a bassinet.

"You mean, he's here — in this room?" I asked. Somehow I thought the hospital would keep him in a separate place and clean him up for a while.

"Uh-huh," said Barney. "In this hospital they let him sleep in the room with your mom."

Barney went to the bassinet and picked him up. Nick looked at him. "He's bald!" he exclaimed.

"Not true," said Barney. He pulled aside the

blanket. Well, he was practically bald.

"Why don't you hold him, Jodi?" Mom asked.

I wasn't ready for this yet. I sat down in a chair. Barney handed him to me. I was afraid of dropping him. His face was kind of wrinkled, and he *was* nearly bald. He hardly had any eyebrows.

Then I looked down at him. His eyes were squinched up as if he were trying to focus on me.

"Hi, Travis," I said.

He didn't say anything, not even a gurgle.

"I'm Jodi. I can do a roundoff back somersault dismount from the beam."

"Quit bragging to him," said Nick, but Mom was grinning at me.

I turned back to Travis. "Look, kid," I whispered, "if you're ever afraid of something, come to me. I'm your big sister. I can help you out."

About the Author

Elizabeth Levy decided that the only way she could write about gymnastics was to try it herself. Besides taking classes she is involved with a group of young gymnasts near her home in New York City, and enjoys following their progress.

Elizabeth Levy's other Apple Paperbacks are *A Different Twist*, *The Computer That Said Steal Me*, and all the other books in THE GYMNASTS series.

She likes visiting schools to give talks and meet her readers. Kids love her presentations. Why? "I do a cartwheel!" says Levy. "At least I try to."

WIN A TRIP TO THE 1991 WORLD GYMNASTICS CHAMPIONSHIPS

We'll send the Winner of this random drawing and his/her parent or guardian (age 21 or older) to the exciting 1991 WORLD GYMNASTICS CHAMPIONSHIPS in Indianapolis, Indiana! The trip includes:

★ Hotel — 3 nights! (September 13, 14 and 15, 1991)
★ Round-trip airline tickets!
★ 2 premium seat tickets to major championship events!

Just fill in the coupon below and return it by May 31, 1991.

Rules: Entries must be postmarked by May 31, 1991. Winner will be picked at random and notified by mail. Parent or guardian must be age 21 or older. No purchase necessary. Valid only in the U.S. Void where prohibited. Taxes on prizes are the responsibility of the winner and his/hers immediate family. Employees of Scholastic Inc.; its agencies, affiliates, subsidiaries; and their immediate families not eligible.

Fill in the coupon or write the information on a 3" x 5" piece of paper and mail to: 1991 WORLD GYMNASTICS CHAMPIONSHIPS, Scholastic Inc., P.O. Box 755, New York, NY 10003.

1991 World Gymnastics Championships

Name _____ Age _____

Street _____

City _____ State _____ Zip _____

Where did you buy this *Gymnasts* book?

☐ Bookstore ☐ Drugstore ☐ Supermarket ☐ Library

☐ Book Club ☐ Book Fair ☐ Other _____ (specify)

GYM790

APPLE® PAPERBACKS

THE GYMNASTS™

by Elizabeth Levy

Available wherever you buy books, or use this order form.

Scholastic Inc., P.O. Box 7502, 2931 East McCarty Street, Jefferson City, MO 65102

Please send me the books I have checked above. I am enclosing $_____ (please add $2.00 to cover shipping and handling). Send check or money order — no cash or C.O.D.s please.

Name _____

Address _____

City _____ State/Zip _____

Please allow four to six weeks for delivery. Offer good in the U.S. only. Sorry, mail orders are not available to residents of Canada. Prices subject to change.

GYM1090

THE BABY-SITTERS CLUB®

by Ann M. Martin

Collect Them All!

The seven girls at Stoneybrook Middle School get into all kinds of adventures...with school, boys, and, of course, baby-sitting!

☐ NI43388-1	#1	Kristy's Great Idea	$2.95
☐ NI43513-2	#2	Claudia and the Phantom Phone Calls	$2.95
☐ NI43511-6	#3	The Truth About Stacey	$2.95
☐ NI42498-X	#30	Mary Anne and the Great Romance	$2.95
☐ NI42497-1	#31	Dawn's Wicked Stepsister	$2.95
☐ NI42496-3	#32	Kristy and the Secret of Susan	$2.95
☐ NI42495-5	#33	Claudia and the Great Search	$2.95
☐ NI42494-7	#34	Mary Anne and Too Many Boys	$2.95
☐ NI42508-0	#35	Stacey and the Mystery of Stoneybrook	$2.95
☐ NI43565-5	#36	Jessi's Baby-sitter	$2.95
☐ NI43566-3	#37	Dawn and the Older Boy	$2.95
☐ NI43567-1	#38	Kristy's Mystery Admirer	$2.95
☐ NI43568-X	#39	Poor Mallory!	$2.95
☐ NI44082-9	#40	Claudia and the Middle School Mystery	$2.95
☐ NI43570-1	#41	Mary Anne Versus Logan	$2.95
☐ NI44083-7	#42	Jessi and the Dance School Phantom	$2.95
☐ NI43571-X	#43	Stacey's Revenge (Apr. '91)	$2.95
☐ NI44240-6		Baby-sitters on Board! Super Special #1	$3.50
☐ NI44239-2		Baby-sitters' Summer Vacation Super Special #2	$3.50
☐ NI43973-1		Baby-sitters' Winter Vacation Super Special #3	$3.50
☐ NI42493-9		Baby-sitters' Island Adventure Super Special #4	$3.50
☐ NI43575-2		California Girls! Super Special #5	$3.50

For a complete listing of all the Baby-sitter Club titles write to:
Customer Service at the address below.

Available wherever you buy books...or use this order form.

Scholastic Inc., P.O. Box 7502, 2931 E. McCarty Street, Jefferson City, MO 65102

Please send me the books I have checked above. I am enclosing $ _____
(please add $2.00 to cover shipping and handling). Send check or money order — no cash or C.O.D.s please.

Name _____

Address _____

City _____ State/Zip _____

Please allow four to six weeks for delivery. Offer good in U.S.A. only. Sorry, mail orders are not available to residents of Canada. Prices subject to change.   BSC790